THE BEAR'S
TOOTHACHE

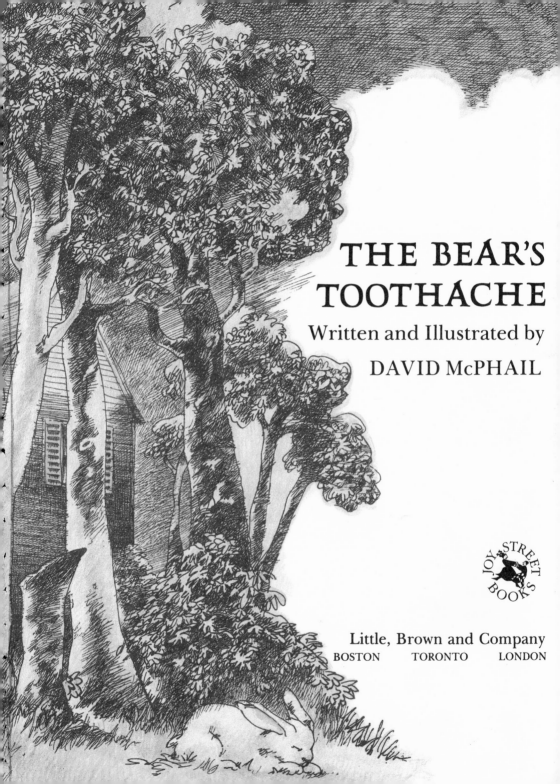

THE BEAR'S TOOTHACHE

Written and Illustrated by

DAVID McPHAIL

Little, Brown and Company
BOSTON   TORONTO   LONDON

LIBRARY OF CONGRESS CATALOG CARD NO. 79-140482

20 19 18 17 16 15 14   (HC)
10 9 8 7 6 5   (PB)

ISBN 0-316-56312-9R (HC)
ISBN 0-316-56325-0 (PB)

*Joy Street Books are published
by Little, Brown and Company (Inc.)*

AHS

*Published simultaneously in Canada
by Little, Brown & Company (Canada) Limited*

PRINTED IN THE UNITED STATES OF AMERICA

For my son, Tristian
for Dr. Katherine Leland
for Dr. Arthur Bernstein
and
for Toughie the Bear

THE BEAR'S TOOTHACHE

One night I heard something
outside my window.

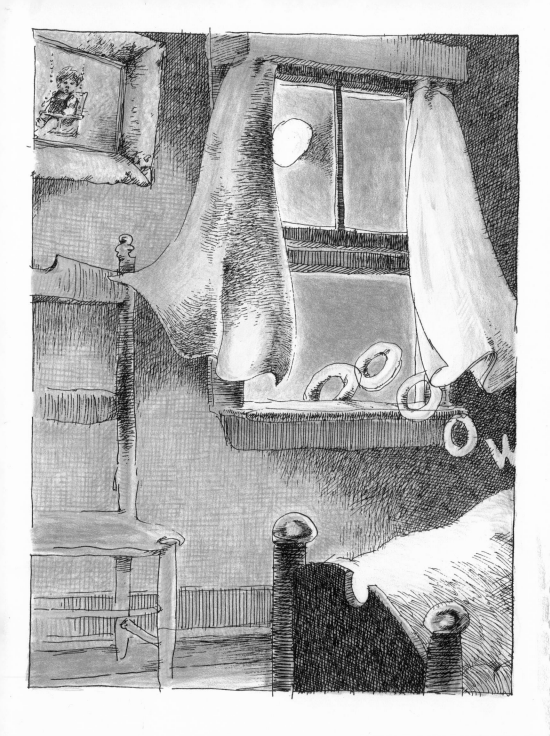

It was a bear

with a toothache.

I invited him in

and examined his teeth.

When I found the one that ached,
I tried to pull it out.

It wouldn't budge.

"Maybe some steak will loosen it
a little," said the bear.
So we went down to the kitchen,
where the bear chewed on some steak
and anything else he could find.

17

Pretty soon the food was all gone,
but the tooth was no looser than before.

When we got back to my room,
I tried to hit the tooth with my pillow.

But the bear ducked,
and I hit the lamp instead
and knocked it to the floor.
Crash!

The noise woke my father,
who got up and came to my room.

"What happened to the lamp?" he asked.

"It fell on the floor," I answered.

"Oh," he said, and he went back to bed.

Then I had a good idea.

I tied one end of my cowboy rope
to the bear's tooth

and tied the other end to the bedpost.

Then the bear stood on the windowsill

and jumped.

And just as he hit the ground,

the tooth popped out!

The bear was so happy that
he gave me the tooth

to put under my pillow.